Dora Sigerson Shorter

Ballads & Poems

Dora Sigerson Shorter

Ballads & Poems

ISBN/EAN: 9783744777193

Printed in Europe, USA, Canada, Australia, Japan

Cover: Foto ©Andreas Hilbeck / pixelio.de

More available books at **www.hansebooks.com**

BALLADS & POEMS
BY DORA SIGERSON
(Mrs CLEMENT SHORTER)

LONDON: JAMES BOWDEN
10 HENRIETTA ST.
1899

Edinburgh : T. and A. CONSTABLE, Printers to Her Majesty

CERTAIN of these verses have appeared in *Blackwood's Magazine, Longman's Magazine, The Spectator, The Daily Chronicle, The Bookman, Cassell's Magazine, The Pall Mall Gazette*, and *The Westminster Gazette*. The writer is indebted to the Editors of these publications.

CONTENTS

I

MY LADY'S SLIPPER
AND OTHER BALLADS

MY LADY'S SLIPPER

A TRUE STORY

I

I AM a man who hath known trouble,
    O'Roork of the Lake.
On my life's glass joy rose as a bubble
    To glitter and break.

She laid in mine her hands long and slender,
    So softly sweet,
Little curls on her head tasselled like tender
    Gold autumn wheat.

Brown leaves around her whirling and falling,
    Blown to her cheek.
I with my heart for her loud in its calling,
    Still could not speak!

Wife of my foe thus pleading before me,
    There seemed no wrong :
With my mad passions that stifled and tore me,
    Who could be strong?

3

What had she shown me there in her weeping,
    On her white arm?
Black, cruel bruises vividly keeping
    Tales of alarm.

What had she begged me there in the morning,
    God judge me well?
What had she said, that I without warning
    Struggled in Hell?

'Take me and save me, be my defender,
    Hide me away.'
She from my old foe bid me befriend her,
    How could I stay?

Here was revenge for the old bitter wronging,
    Here to my hand;
Here was the love of my life—of my longing,
    Could I withstand?

Thrice did I turn to fly from my danger,
    God judge me true,
Vowed that my love to her love was a stranger,
    This did I do.

But when I looked on her, heard her calling,
    Kneeling so low,

There the sun's sheen on golden locks falling,
    How could I go?

Dearly beloved, shaken with sorrow,
    Branded with blows,
Which way does honour lie? think! for to-morrow
    Only God knows!

One man should use her so, he in whose keeping
    Broken she lay;
One man should love her so, see her weeping,
    And turn away.

He were inhuman.   Riding behind me
    Home did she speed.
Which way did honour lie?   Love did so blind me,
    Great was her need.

There at my door did I linger awhile
    Tending my horse,
Saw her flit up the long steps, and her smile
    Bore no remorse.

On her pale brow was a look of soft peace,
    Upward she went;
Never a glance in her welcome release
    Backward she bent.

Red was her cloak, and her face like a flower
    Dear to behold ;
Little red slippers she wore in that hour
    Buckled with gold.

Up the white steps like a flash of red flame,
    In through the door ;
Quick did I follow to tremble her name —
    Saw her no more.

Saw her no more from that day — she had gone,
    Vanished away,
Like a bright light on my pathway that shone,
    Then let me stray.

II

I had a neighbour—he was my friend,
    Since in the wood
Lone our two houses were, each gable-end
    United stood.

This was a manor once built for a knight
    In days of old,

But with the centuries love and their fight
        Squandered the gold.

So for my friend, when inheritance came
        Coffers were bare,
Just the old keep and the weight of a name,
        This was his share.

Then he divided the house into two—
        I took a part.
Now in my grief for his guidance I flew,
        Knowing his heart.

'At dawn he departed,' the little page said.—
        Time without end.
Oh, on what broken wings laggard hours fled!
        He was my friend.

So the years passed me and shed in their flight
        Dust and decay ;
Ruin and rust on the old manor clings,
        Crumbling away.

Only my desolate chambers remain,
        Racked by the wind ;
All down the years go I seeking in vain—
        Never to find.

Vanished my love—my friend—not a cry!
            Leaving life's race,
Like the bright meteors that slip in the sky,
            Leap into space.

III

The shadows are long, I crouch by the fire,
            Bitter with years,
See all the shades of my former desire
            Ghostly through tears.

Down the long hall to me, weary of play,
            Comes my young hound;
At my feet, tumbled, his dusty toy lay—-
            What had he found?

There in the firelight glitter of gold,
            God make me strong!
A little red slipper I trembling hold,
            Lost for so long.

So musty and faded, mouldy with years,
            Where hidden and how!

Here, after searching, much passion and tears,
    Come to me now.

'What is in hiding? Oh, track me the way—
    Find her, my hound!'
Up the steep stairs he goes, eager for play,
    Gambolling around.

Up to the turret room, close to the wall,
    Barking he goes;
Tears till the wainscoting crumbling falls
    Under his blows.

Rotten with age, here a panel unseen
    Slips 'neath my hand;
Into the silence of love that has been,
    I shuddering stand.

This is the secret hidden away,
    Built in the wall—
Between the two houses a room cold and grey,
    Gloomy and small.

Huddled and crumbling, stretched on the ground,
    Mould and decay;
Dust to dust mingled, the secret is found,
    So here they lay.

In one embrace down the desolate years
    Over my head
Did they lie smiling and know of my tears,
    Cruel and dead.

Here the grey spider had circled them o'er,
    Hand to hand tied,
In their clasped fingers lay hidden his store,
    There, too, he spied.

I was the fool then who linked in that clasp
    Each skeleton hand ;
Thus !—will I be he who loosens the grasp,
    How was it planned ?

Here is a phial : was death then so sweet,
    Honour or life ?
This was the only way lovers could meet—
    She was a wife.

Wrapped in death's silence, safe from my scorn ;
    He was my friend :
It was *his* love whom I bore home that morn,
    His to the end !

Was it the woman who plotted and spied,
    Using my heart

Just for a stone there to step where the tide
    Kept them apart?

Was he a coward, lying lowly to wait,
    Giving me blame?
Vain do I strike him, avenging my fate.
    Cursed be his name!

She was my love: did she bid him believe
    I for his sake
Cast away honour to stoop and deceive,
    Bore *him* the stake?

He was my friend: dare I doubt him and know?
    What if it be
Nothing he knew of her coming—the blow
    That fell on me?

Knowing his honour, it might be she came,
    Since he was still.
What did she care for my torture or shame?—
    I served her will.

Knowing his weakness under her eyes,
    Boldly she flew
Into his arms, hushed his blame and surprise,
    If this be true.

Speak to me once, for God's sake, till I know
  What was the worst!
My friend, my beloved, did you both plan the blow
  Made me accurst?

Speak to me once, O dear voices, for I
  Wait to forgive!
Tell me your secret: the echoes reply—
  I alone live.

　　　　.　　　　　　.　　　.

Only the bark of my dog in the tower,
  Glad in his play;
' Red was her cloak, and her face like a flower ';
  Hide it away!

THE PHANTOM DEER

'Do you hunt alone to-day, O Red Richard!
  Pray you tell me, do you hunt all your lone?'
'Ay, I am for the chase, little cousin,
  And wish no other spearing save my own.'

'And whither are you going, O Red Richard!
  That I may from the terrace watch your way?'
'All deep within the magic woods of Toonagh,
  It is there that my hunting is to-day.'

He vaulted to the saddle of his palfrey,
  And laid across his arm the bridle-rein;
And he drew her to his knee, all fair and rosy,
  Laughed—'A kiss, child, to bring me home again.'

Then he rode on all so gay, so forgetting,
  His light kiss as a flame upon her cheek;
But she went back alone into her chamber,
  There to weep like her tender heart should break.

'O my love! though you love me not, Red Richard,
    As you ride with your heart all whole and gay '—
She drew from her breast a magic potion,
    Saying, 'Sweet will your hunting be to-day.

'Three drops for you I drink, O Cousin Richard!
    Three drops that you may have your heart's desire;
As a white deer I shall spring the paths before you,
    Right merry shall you follow till you tire.'

Now came upon the pathway of Red Richard,
    As he rode through the arbours of the wood,
A white doe, so beautiful and trembling,
    That all disarmed and wondering he stood.

'Very sweet you are and fair,' said Red Richard,
    'Pretty doe, like a woman soft and white;
I could swear they were the dark eyes of my cousin
    That gaze with the sad mystery of night.'

Then he laughed, and the deer, all quickly turning,
    Sprang before him through the glades deep and
        green;
Hot, he followed with his spear ever ready—
    Oh, such hunting as this was never seen!

He followed her so fast by stream and valley,
   He followed her so close through bog and briar ;
Thrice she lured him round the woods by his castle,
   But vanished ere he had his red desire.

And he rode home so slow and heavy-hearted,
   And from his weary steed he flung him down ;
There he saw on the terrace watching for him
   A little maid all clad in snowy gown.

And he cried, 'Come you hither, little cousin,
   I swear that it was one as fair as you,
Clad in white, with her eyes as dark and splendid,
   Who has fooled so me the glowing morning
      through.

'I promise to you, pretty,' laughed Red Richard,
   'To-morrow I shall bring her to your feet' ;
Then she said, smiling low, the little cousin,
   'Oh, to-morrow may your hunting be as sweet!'

When the dawn was pale and young came Red
      Richard
   Through his castle gate into the magic wood ;
And there upon his path, so fair and trembling,
   The slender doe all palpitating stood

And he chased her then by rock and by river,
   He chased her long by meadow and by hill:
Thrice she took him through the gardens of his
     castle,
   But she vanished ere his spear had had its will.

And so home, foiled and furious, rode Red Richard;
   He flung himself all weary in his chair,
And beside him came the white little maiden,
   Saying, 'Cousin, was your hunting very fair?'

Then he laughed.   'But to-morrow I shall win her,
   Though she go where no foot has ever been.
To your feet will I bring her, pretty cousin;
   Oh, such hunting as mine was never seen!'

Up at dawn, glad and eager, rose Red Richard;
   The quickest steed in all the land had he,
And he rode to the magic woods of Toonagh—
   There the white doe was grazing peacefully.

And then upon the tender moss behind her,
   So softly and so swiftly did he ride,
That she bounded but a pace from her resting
   Ere his hot spear was red within her side.

And he tracked her through the mist and through
    shadow,
He followed the wet crimson on his way;
And he vowed he would have her dead or living,
    Or follow her until the Judgment Day.

All red was the pathway to his castle,
    And all eager and all fierce was his quest,
Till he came upon the corpse of his cousin—
    Found his sharp spear was buried in her breast.

.   .   .   .   .   .

So it is that the magic woods of Toonagh
    Are haunted by the spirit of a deer:
She wanders by the castle of Red Richard—
    Within her side the wounding of a spear.

JEANNE BRAS: A BALLAD OF SORROW

' JEANNE BRAS! Jeanne Bras! arise and let me in;
　Jeanne Bras! Jeanne Bras! will you awake?'
' *Now who comes so late at my door, her way to win,*
　Who knocks thus my slumbering to break?'

' Oh! it is your child who is ill with bitter woe!
　So open to her the bolted door.'
' *I had a child, but she left me long ago:*
　I pray you to trouble me no more.'

' Oh! one stands here — she is weary unto death,
　Beaten with the wind and with the rain.'
' *The child I bore I shall curse with dying breath,*
　And so your knocking is in vain.'

' Your child is here, with her bowed and humbled
　　head
　Grown grey while yet its years are green.'
　18

' *My child had hair gold as a silkworm's thread,*
   She held it as high as a queen.'

' One cries here, and her lips, so sad and white,
   Still call you in a daughter's name.'
' *My child's mouth bore a smile of fond delight ;*
   They never had pleaded of shame.'

' One weeps here : in her eyes joy's flame is stilled,
   And she on her mother doth cry.'
' *My child's eyes with God's innocence were filled,*
   And pure with the blue of His sky.'

' Here is your child ; her weak and weary feet
   Have led her to her mother's door.'
' *My child stole from my side all gladly fleet ;*
   I tell you to trouble me no more.'

' O mother, mother ! a little babe I bring ;
   I pray you rise and let us through.'
' *On my child's hand was set no wedding-ring ;*
   I shall not open unto you.'

' Oh, cruel you are !   Unforgiving to your child :
   Sorrow and shame make her appeal.'
' *Did she think of me when a stranger came and smiled ?*
   She went like a dog to his heel !'

‘ A priest ! a priest, I pray you bring to me ;
    Unchurched and unshriven am I.’
‘ *As you went, you shall go, unblessed to be.*
    Why do you linger here to cry ? ’

‘ A priest !   A priest !   My little dying boy !
    Unchristened and unholy he lies.’
‘ *Accurst your sorrow, accurst your joy—*
    Begone !   I will answer not your cries.’

   .   .   .   .

Jeanne Bras, Jeanne Bras, she rose up with the dawn,
    And flung off the bolt and the chain :
The first thing she rested her hot eyes upon
    Was the child who had called her in vain.

The next thing she saw was the babe, all so white,
    Lying cold on its cold mother’s breast.
Each face bore the tears of its pitiful plight—
    They lay in their sleeping unblest.

Jeanne Bras, Jeanne Bras, she laid them side by side,
    All in their cold and silent bed ;
Then she knelt by their grave, and all bitterly she
        cried
    Till the stars trembled forth overhead.

Now they lay all cold and they lay all still
  Till the night of the third long day ;
Then they rose in their grave-clothes, all stiff and chill,
  And back to her door made their way.

' Jeanne Bras ! Jeanne Bras ! arise and let us through ;
  Jeanne Bras ! Jeanne Bras ! will you awake ? '
' Oh glad, sweet ghost, will I free my door to you,
  And pray your forgiveness to take !'

Jeanne Bras arose, and she lit her taper bright,
  And her door she did set open wide :
She heard a young child go crying in the night,
  But never a one was outside.

She prayed till dawn, and wept the lone, long day,
  Weary she laid her down to rest ;
There came to her door a ghost all pale and grey,
  A babe lying cold on her breast.

' Jeanne Bras ! Jeanne Bras ! give shelter !   Oh,
      awake !
  Chill we are, and bitter is our woe.'
' O child, dear child, your mother's heart doth break,
  While cold and unsheltered you go !'

She rose up straight, and bright her taper shone
 As she opened the door so wide;
But alas! to her grief, the woful ghost had gone,
 And never a one was outside.

Jeanne Bras, so pale, she mounted up her stair,
 And no tear did she now let fall;
But she laid her down on her pallet hard and bare,
 And her white face she turned to the wall.

She lay there all night, she lay the day through,
 And never a word spoke she,
Till there came with the dark a sad weeping she knew
 The cry of her daughter to be.

She tossed to the left, she tossed to the right,
 The sound could not stifle nor still;
She heard the loud wail of a woman's sad plight,
 And a babe in its agony shrill.

Again she rose up with her taper aflame,
 And the great door all soon she unbarred;
She called through the night on her lost daughter's
  name,
 She went to the ancient churchyard.

Feeble she was and all old with her years,
  By her child's grave she bent her white head ;
And her poor heart it broke with the burden of tears,
  And she lay there as cold as the dead.

    .   .   .   .   .

Her ghost it still walks through the dark hours of
        night,
  She signs with the grief of the wind ;
She holds in her hand a wax taper all white ;
  She seeks what she never will find.

THE WHITE WITCH

Heaven help your home to-night,
M'Cormac, for I know
A white witch woman is your bride :
You married for your woe.

You thought her but a simple maid
That roamed the mountain-side ;
She put the witch's glance on you,
And so became your bride.

But I have watched her close and long,
And know her all too well ;
I never churned before her glance
But evil luck befell.

Last week the cow beneath my hand
Gave out no milk at all ;
I turned, and saw the pale-haired girl
Lean laughing by the wall.

21

'A little sup,' she cried, 'for me;
The day is hot and dry.'
'Begone!' I said, 'you witch's child,'
She laughed a loud good-bye.

And when the butter in the churn
Will never rise, I see
Beside the door the white witch girl
Has got her eyes on me.

At dawn to-day I met her out
Upon the mountain-side,
And all her slender finger-tips
Were each a crimson dyed.

Now I had gone to seek a lamb
The darkness sent astray:
Sore for a lamb the dawning winds
And sharp-beaked birds of prey.

But when I saw the white witch maid
With blood upon her gown,
I said, 'I'm poorer by a lamb;
The witch has dragged it down.'

And, 'Why is this, your hands so red
All in the early day?'

I seized her by the shoulder fair,
She pulled herself away.

' It is the raddle on my hands,
The raddle all so red,
For I have marked M'Cormac's sheep
And little lambs,' she said.

' And what is this upon your mouth
And on your cheek so white ? '
' Oh, it is but the berries' stain ' ;
She trembled in her fright.

' I swear it is no berries' stain,
Nor raddle all so red' ;
I laid my hands about her throat,
She shook me off, and fled.

I had not gone to follow her
A step upon the way,
When came I to my own lost lamb,
That dead and bloody lay.

' Come back,' I cried, ' you witch's child,
Come back and answer me' ;
But no maid on the mountain-side
Could ever my eyes see.

I looked into the glowing east,
I looked into the south,
But did not see the slim young witch,
With crimson on her mouth.

Now, though I looked both well and long,
And saw no woman there,
Out from the bushes by my side
There crept a snow-white hare.

With knife in hand I followed it
By ditch, by bog, by hill :
I said, ' Your luck be in your feet,
For I shall do you ill.'

I said, ' Come, be you fox or hare,
Or be you mountain maid,
I 'll cut the witch's heart from you,
For mischief you have made.'

She laid her spells upon my path,
The brambles held and tore,
The pebbles slipped beneath my feet,
The briars wounded sore.

And then she vanished from my eyes
Beside M'Cormac's farm,

I ran to catch her in the house
And keep the man from harm.

She stood with him beside the fire,
And when she saw my knife,
She flung herself upon his breast
And prayed he 'd save her life.

' The woman is a witch,' I cried,
' So cast her off from you ' ;
' She 'll be my wife to-day,' he said,
' Be careful what you do! '

' The woman is a witch,' I said ;
He laughed both loud and long :
She laid her arms about his neck,
Her laugh was like a song.

' The woman is a witch,' he said,
And laughed both long and loud ;
She bent her head upon his breast,
Her hair was like a cloud.

I said, ' See blood upon her mouth
And on each finger-tip ! '
He said, ' I see a pretty maid,
A rose upon her lip.'

He took her slender hand in his
To kiss the stain away—
Oh, well she cast her spell on him,
What could I do but pray?

'May Heaven guard your house to-night!'
I whisper as I go,
'For you have won a witch for bride,
And married for your woe.'

THE FETCH: A BALLAD

' WHAT makes you so late at the trysting?
What caused you so long to be?
For a weary time I have waited
From the hour you promised me.'

' I would I were here by your side, love,
Full many an hour ago,
For a thing I passed on the roadway
All mournful and so slow.'

' And what have you passed on the roadside
That kept you so long and late?'
' It is weary the time behind me
Since I left my father's gate.

' As I hastened on in the gloaming
By the road to you to-night,
There I saw the corpse of a young maid
All clad in a shroud of white.'

30

'And was she some comrade cherished,
Or was she a sister dead,
That you left thus your own true lover
Till the trysting-hour had fled?'

'Oh, I would that I could discover,
But her face was turned away,
And I knew I must turn and follow
Wherever her resting lay.'

'And did it go up by the town path,
Did it go down by the lake?
I know there are but the two churchyards
Where a corpse its rest may take.'

'They did not go up by the town path,
Nor stopped by the lake their feet,
They buried the corpse all silently
Where the four cross-roads do meet.'

'And was it so strange a sight, then,
That you should go like a child,
Thus to leave me wait all forgotten,
By a passing sight beguiled?'

'' Twas my name that I heard them whisper,
Each mourner that passed by me;

And I had to follow their footsteps,
Though their faces I could not see.'

'And right well I should like to know, now,
Who might be this fair young maid,
So come with me, my own true love,
If you be not afraid.'

He did not go down by the lakeside,
He did not go by the town,
But carried her to the four cross-roads,
And he there did set her down.

'Now, I see no track of a foot here,
I see no mark of a spade,
And I know right well in this white road
That never a grave was made.'

And he took her hand in his right hand
And led her to town away,
And there he questioned the good old priest,
Did he bury a maid that day.

And he took her hand in his right hand,
Down to the church by the lake,
And there he questioned the fair young priest
If a maiden her life did take.

But neither had heard of a new grave
In all the parish around,
And no one could tell of a young maid
Thus put in unholy ground.

So he loosed her hand from his hand,
And turned on his heel away,
And, 'I know now you are false,' he said,
'From the lie you told to-day.'

And she said, ' Alas! what evil thing
Did to-night my senses take? '
She knelt her down by the water-side
And wept as her heart would break.

And she said, ' Oh, what fairy sight then
Was it thus my grief to see?
I will sleep well 'neath the still water,
Since my love has turned from me.'

And her love he went to the north land,
And far to the south went he,
And her distant voice he still could hear
Call weeping so bitterly.

And he could not rest in the daytime
He could not sleep in the night,

So he hastened back to the old road,
With the trysting-place in sight.

What first he heard was his own love's name,
And keening both loud and long,
What first he saw was his love's dear face,
At the head of a mourning throng.

And all white she was as the dead are,
And never a move made she,
But passed him by on her lone black pall,
Still sleeping so peacefully.

And all cold she was as the dead are,
And never a word she spake,
When they said, ' Unholy is her grave
For she her life did take.'

And silent she was as the dead are,
And never a cry she made,
When there came, more sad than the keening,
The ring of a digging spade.

No rest she had in the old town church,
No grave by the lake so sweet,
They buried her in unholy ground,
Where the four cross-roads do meet.

THE FATE OF THE THREE SONS OF UISNEACH AND DEIRDRÉ, DAUGHTER OF FEILIM

Woe to thee, daughter of Feilim! woe to thee,
    Deirdré!

Slain for thy sake were the three sons of Uisneach,
    and red

Grew the broad plains of Ulster, on Connaught
    unnumbered the dead.

Woe to thee, Deirdré!—Deirdré, daughter of Feilim.

Smiled the sweet babe in the face of the Druid and
    his warning,

Held her young mouth for his kissing, and wept at
    his scorning.

'King Connor, there's woe for thy pity, this woman-
    child born,

This bud of sweet promise, will wound herself red
    with her thorn.

O King, in the future I prophesy evil before thee,

With the life of this child. Wilt thou listen and heed
    to my story?

The breath of a babe? or Connaught and Ulster in
    sorrow ?

Let her be slain !   Who remembers the deed on to-
    morrow ? '

A dozen swords spring from their scabbards and flash
    fierce and bright,

The child for the fair steel stretched out her small
    hands in delight.

Connor laughed : ' Let her live, and if beauty should
    grant her a dower,

I will wed.   Toast your queen, ere I hide her from
    fate in a tower.'

So the child prattled and grew fair as a wild-flower
    uncurled,

Till the maid's reason began to wonder how narrow
    her world,

What the great walls of the court hid from her in-
    quisitive view,

What perfumed the wind from the west, and where
    went the finch when he flew.

Many sweet tales told her nurse, that fed her romantic
    young brain,

Till sleeping were sweet for its dreams, and waking
    was dreaming again.

What if their lone tower was built on a high rock
    right out in the sea,

Like the rock in that fountain of hers ? or perhaps, it
    might be

The world were a garden of flowers.   Comes a prince
    in a boat—

That dream-prince of hers—(thrice a raven, with
    threatening note,

Flaps his wings)—or mayhap on an elf steed he 'd ride.

High walls could not stay him.   She leaned from her
    casement and cried :

'Look, nurse, they have slain a young deer in the
    courtyard below,

And the raven awaits them.   My prince shall have
    skin like yon snow,

As red as that blood be his lip, and his hair like the
    raven's black wing.'

'Hush, dearest !' the woman replied.   'Hush, dearest,
    and think on the King !'

'Oh, nurse, were the pretty flower safe to live on the
    ocean's broad breast ?

Would the little wren fly for her home and her mate
    to the eagle's cold nest ? '

'Peace, childie ! last night the wolf-hound howled
    long 'neath thy window-sill there.'

'Sweet nurse ! dost thou know of a youth, so pure-
    skinned, with raven dark hair ? '

'Peace, child ! know the death-watch ticked night
    long at thy own bed-head,

And a cock crew thrice out of hours.'   'Oh, nurse !
    and with lips blood-red ? '

' Darling, in Connor's famed court, I 've heard of as
    fair a young knight.'
' Oh, nurse ! I 've loved him in dreams.—Wilt bring
    him but once to my sight?'

Woe to thee, fair child of sorrow !   Love laughs at
    high walls in derision.
Woe to Naois and Ainlé and Ardan, who rescued thee
    safe from thy prison.
Into the mouth of the lion they flew from the lion
    pursuing,
For Scotia's king saw the bride's face—loved the
    beauty that was her undoing,
And many were slain for her sake, till the brave sons
    of Ulster have spoken :
' Lo. King ! it were sad, for one maid that our armies
    were scattered and broken.'
And Connor, aloud, to those chiefs, bade the three
    sons of Uisneach return·
Forgiven, come home to their land.   But his heart was
    still hot with the burn
Of the shame of the maiden's desertion, and her scorn
    of a king and his glory ;
He thought that the lips of the world must be glad on
    the theme of his story.

Tricked by a girl! how his pride turned the word,
    till Hate made it, in growing,

Fly back to the Druid and his warning. So this was
    the seed of his sowing.

He half thought it was writ on his brow, that the
    people were sick of their laughter;

He turned the stone in his sleeve : ' Let them laugh ;
    he laughs best who laughs after.'

So Eogan, at word of the King, when he heard that
    the three youths had landed,

Was to welcome the brothers to Erinn, outspoken to
    seem and free-handed—

' But '—this in a whisper aside—' slay them, each man,
    without warning.'

So by the sword of a traitor fell Ainlé, Ardan, and
    Naois, for scorning

Of a king by the daughter of Feilim ; and Deirdré
    was brought to King Connor.

What heeded she of his laughter, the sneers or the
    slights put upon her?

Since Naois was dead, her belovèd, the rose on her
    cheek paled with sorrow,

And laughter was dead on her lips, only tears were
    her own night and morrow,

Till the King a new vengeance had planned to wake
    her strange listlessness to life :

To Eogan, the slayer of Naois, he gave the sad
    Deirdré to wife.

And Deirdré smiled once in his face as she mounted
    the steed by his side,

That was chafing to bear her away and bring the
    false Eogan his bride.

Never such quarry was seen as Connor's men hunted
    that day,

Never such laughter was heard as they followed up
    valley and brae,

For Connor the King for his vengeance was spending
    his courser's hot breath,

But Deirdré, the daughter of Feilim, was racing her
    brown steed for Death.

Woe to thee, daughter of Feilim! woe to thee,
    Deirdré!

Slain for thy sake were the fair sons of Uisneach, and
    red

Grew the broad plains of Ulster, on Connaught un-
    numbered the dead—

Woe to thee, Deirdré, Deirdré, daughter of Feilim!

FALSE DEARBHORGIL [1]

Woe to the House of Breffni, and to Red O'Ruark
    woe!

Woe to us all in Erin for the shame that laid us low!

And cursed be you, Dearbhorgil, who severed north
    and south,

And ruin brought to Erin with the smiling of your
    mouth.

.   .   .   .

It is the Prince of Breffni rides quick in the pale of day,

Deep in his eyes a shadow, a frown on his forehead
    lay;

And spur and bit not sparing, he rests nor horse nor
    page,

But rides into his castle like a man who wins a wage.

The Prince of Breffni suspects that his wife Dearbhorgil has a lover.

[1] Dearbhorgil was the daughter of the King of Meath and the wife of O'Ruark, Prince of Breffni. She was beloved of Macmurrah, King of Leinster, who is reported to have met her in secret and to have won her affections. Macmurrah carried her off, but in the subsequent war of revenge was defeated, and fled to England. His appeal to Henry II. of Anjou led to the invasion and conquest of Ireland by Strongbow and other Anglo-Norman adventurers.

And up the twisting staircase, into his lady's room,
He strides with paling forehead, like a man to meet
    his doom,
But from his lady's chamber he comes with sobbing
    breath,
With a joy upon his white lips, like a man escaped
    from death.

' And shame be mine, Dearbhorgil,' beneath his beard
    said he,
' That I should stoop to listen to a slander told to me.
And shame be mine, Macmurrah, that I should half
    believe
You could be false to kingship by stooping to deceive.'

But in the lady's chamber the little page did frown,
And on his cheek so crimson the bitter tears fell
    down.
' And false she is and cruel, to a knight so brave and
    true,
And I wot now she is distant, thus leaving him the
    rue.

' I wot now she is riding far upon her palfrey white,
And the comrade beside her is not her own true
    knight—

A plague upon all women, from north to sunny south,
Since my lips are dumb to honour for the smiling of
　　her mouth!'

But O'Ruark went out right gladly for the lie the page
　　had said,
How his lady still lay resting so weary on her bed;
And he went out to the terrace to cool his fevered
　　cheek,
There he saw his kern a-watching, like one afraid to
　　speak.

O'Ruark goes on the terrace to quiet his unrest before he seeks his lady, and while there his doubts are again awakened.

'What see you from your tower now, O kern?' he
　　turned and cried.
'I see one on the near hills upon a king's horse
　　ride.'
'What see you from your watch, kern: does nothing
　　else appear?'
'There hides one on the terrace, with her eyes all
　　full of fear.'

'And who are you in hiding, who goes 'neath this
　　late moon?'
'I am your true Dearbhorgil, glad home you are thus
　　soon.'

He discovers his wife upon the terrace, where she has hid to watch for her lover.

' No hour for wives to ramble : but wherefore do you
     weep ? '

' With joy for your returning—I wandered in my
     sleep.'

She pre-
tends she
has walked
in her sleep
and is sad
for a
dream's
sake.

' Joy's tears are summer rain, Queen—your eyes are
     sad and red.'

' A dream of evil-boding, and that was all my dread.'

' What was the dream distressful that made your face
     so white ? '

' I dreamt that storm and thunder surrounded you
     to-night.'

He tries to
draw her
into a con-
fession,
having seen
the King of
Leinster
riding on a
white
charger.

' My lady, storm and thunder ride on the near hill's
     side.'

' Then hasten into shelter ! ' the lady paled and
     cried.

' In from the lash of tempest I dare not turn to go,

Lest, coming up from Leinster, it might lay Ulster
     low.'

She will not
understand
him, and
tries to
draw him to
her and
into the
castle.

' My lord, the moon is paling, the dawn grows calm
     and clear.

There is no angry weather, and wherefore do you
     fear ? '

'My lady, hush! the kern sees something on the
    way.'
'My lord, why listen to him?—I have such news to
    say.'

'Nay, I shall hearken to him. O kern, what do you
    see?
If there's aught on the highroad, now quickly tell to
    me.'
'I see one by the pine-wood come on a charger
    white,
He seeks the shadow always, as though he fears the
    light.'

He does not listen, and is full of anger. The kern says he sees a stranger on the highway.

'Half-blind the kern, and aged, all wizen, cold, and
    grey.
A wolf is on the highroad, who hurries quick away.'
'A wolf, Queen, is a danger who in the shade does
    go,
At the thief who seeks the night-time I quick shall
    bend my bow.'

She tries to persuade the prince it is a wild dog.

                       (*She screams.*)

'Why did you call, Dearbhorgil, disturbing so my
    aim?'
'My bodkin pierced me sorely, and that is all my
    blame.'

The prince raises his crossbow, and she screams a warning.

'Then, cry out not so loudly, lest he should turn away.'

'My lord has but to bid me, and ever I obey.'

She tries to outwit him again, and uses all her charms, but the prince is not to be blinded.

'Look, kern, again, and answer, where creeps the
    lone wolf now?'

'I see a king's plume waving by yonder oak-tree's
    bough.'

'It is a hawk he watches, that is hanging there so low.'

'Then at that bird of evil, dark death, I'll bend my
    bow.'

                    (She screams.)

She screams again, and her lover, knowing the warning, flies.

'Again you call, Dearbhorgil, and you would have
    him hear?'

'A bat that flew across me was all that made me fear.'

'The wolf speeds down the highroad all at your
    lady's cry,

The hawk has spread his dark wings, and seeks
    another sky.'

Now that the danger is past she soon flatters the prince into believing she loves him alone.

'Why should we heed the grey hawk?—Let him fly
    off to his nest:

Why should we heed the lone wolf?—Let him go in
    peace to rest.'

'My lady, neither beast nor bird slunk round my
    home to-night;

It is a high and honoured prince who rides away in
    fright.'

'And wherefore should you wax so pale, if beast or
    king it be,
Since I have but one prince, and he stands all so
    wroth with me?
There, let the blind kern find his kings in wolf, or
    hawk, or dove,
But come you from the cold, my lord, into your lady's
    love.'

And therefore, as we do believe that which we most
    would fain,
She wooed suspicion from him, and had his heart
    again.
But the little page went sighing, 'A plague may
    women win—
She has put the anger from him with the dimples in
    her chin.'

Woe to the House of Breffni, and to the red O'Ruark
    woe!
And woe to us in Erin for the shame which laid us
    low!
And cursed be you, Dearbhorgil, who eloped into the
    south,
And war made loud in Erin with the smiling of your
    mouth.

But the curse fell heavy on Ireland of her foul dishonour.

II

IRELAND, AND OTHER POEMS

D

IRELAND

'Twas the dream of a God,
  And the mould of His hand,
That you shook 'neath His stroke,
That you trembled and broke
  To this beautiful land.

Here He loosed from His hand
  A brown tumult of wings,
Till the wind on the sea
Bore the strange melody
  Of an island that sings.

He made you all fair,
  You in purple and gold,
You in silver and green,
Till no eye that has seen
  Without love can behold.

I have left you behind
  In the path of the past,
With the white breath of flowers,
With the best of God's hours,
  I have left you at last.

THE WIND ON THE HILLS

Go not to the hills of Erin
When the night winds are about,
Put up your bar and shutter,
And so keep the danger out.

For the good-folk whirl within it,
And they pull you by the hand,
And they push you on the shoulder,
Till you move to their command.

And lo! you have forgotten
What you have known of tears,
And you will not remember
That the world goes full of years;

A year there is a lifetime,
And a second but a day,
And an older world will meet you
Each morn you come away.

60

Your wife grows old with weeping,
And your children one by one
Grow grey with nights of watching,
Before your dance is done.

And it will chance some morning
You will come home no more,
Your wife sees but a withered leaf
In the wind about the door.

And your children will inherit
The unrest of the wind,
They shall seek some face elusive.
And some land they never find.

When the wind is loud, they sighing
Go with hearts unsatisfied,
For some joy beyond remembrance,
For some memory denied.

And all your children's children,
They cannot sleep or rest,
When the wind is out in Erin
And the sun is in the West.

THE LONE OF SOUL

THE world has many lovers, but the one
    She loves the best is he within whose heart
She but half-reigning queen and mistress is :
    Whose lonely soul for ever stands apart,

Who from her face will ever turn away,
    Who but half-hearing listens to her voice,
Whose heart beats to her passion, but whose soul
    Within her presence never will rejoice.

What land has let the dreamer from its gates,
    What face belovèd hides from him away ?
A dreamer outcast from some world of dreams—
    He goes for ever lonely on his way.

The wedded body and the single soul,
    Beside his mate he shall most mateless stand,
For ever to dream of that unseen face—
    For ever to sigh for that enchanted land.

Like a great pine upon some Alpine height,
  Torn by the winds and bent beneath the snow,
Half overthrown by icy avalanche,
  The lone of soul throughout the world must go.

Alone among his kind he stands alone,
  Torn by the passions of his own strange heart,
Stoned by continual wreckage of his dreams,
  He in the crowd for ever is apart.

Like the great pine that, rocking no sweet nest,
  Swings no young birds to sleep upon the bough,
But where the raven only comes to croak—
  ' There lives no man more desolate than thou ! '

So goes the lone of soul amid the world—
  No love upon his breast, with singing, cheers ;
But sorrow builds her home within his heart,
  And, nesting there, will rear her brood of tears.

THE BANSHEE

Now God between us and all harm,
　　For I to-night have seen
A banshee in the shadow pass
　　Along the dark boreen.

And as she went she keened and cried
　　And combed her long white hair,
She stopped at Molly Reilly's door,
　　And sobbed till midnight there.

And is it for himself she moans,
　　Who is so far away?
Or is it Molly Reilly's death
　　She cries until the day?

Now Molly thinks her man is gone
　　A sailor lad to be ;
She puts a candle at her door
　　Each night for him to see.

But he is off to Galway town,
    (And who dare tell her this?)
Enchanted by a woman's eyes,
    Half-maddened by her kiss.

So as we go by Molly's door
    We look towards the sea,
And say, 'May God bring home your lad,
    Wherever he may be.'

I pray it may be Molly's self,
    The banshee keens and cries,
For who dare breathe the tale to her,
    Be it her man who dies?

But there is sorrow on the way,
    For I to-night have seen
A banshee in the shadow pass
    Along the dark boreen.

ALL SOULS' NIGHT

[There is a superstition in some parts of Ireland that the dead
are allowed to return to earth on the 2nd of November (All
Souls' Night), and the peasantry leave food and fire for their
comfort, and set a chair by the hearth for their resting before
they themselves retire to bed.]

O MOTHER, mother, I swept the hearth, I set his chair
    and the white board spread,
I prayed for his coming to our kind Lady when Death's
    sad doors would let out the dead ;
A strange wind rattled the window-pane, and down
    the lane a dog howled on ;
I called his name, and the candle flame burnt dim,
    pressed a hand the door-latch upon.
Deelish ! Deelish ! my woe for ever that I could not
    sever coward flesh from fear.
I called his name, and the pale Ghost came ; but I was
    afraid to meet my dear.
O mother, mother, in tears I checked the sad hours
    past of the year that 's o'er,
Till by God's grace I might see his face and hear the
    sound of his voice once more ;

The chair I set from the cold and wet, he took when
    he came from unknown skies

Of the land of the dead, on my bent brown head I felt
    the reproach of his saddened eyes ;

I closed my lids on my heart's desire, crouched by
    the fire, my voice was dumb :

At my clean-swept hearth he had no mirth, and at my
    table he broke no crumb.

Deelish ! Deelish ! my woe for ever that I could not
    sever coward flesh from fear.

His chair put aside when the young cock cried, and I
    was afraid to meet my dear.

THE ONE FORGOTTEN

A SPIRIT speeding down on All Souls' Eve
From the wide gates of that mysterious shore
Where sleep the dead, sung softly and yet sweet.
'So gay a wind was never heard before,'
The old man said, and listened by the fire ;
And, ' 'Tis the souls that pass us on their way,'
The young maids whispered, clinging side by side,
So left their glowing nuts a while to pray.

Still the pale spirit, singing through the night,
Came to this window, looking from the dark
Into the room ; then passing to the door
Where crouched the whining dog, afraid to bark,
Tapped gently without answer, pressed the latch,
Pushed softly open, and then tapped once more.
The maidens cried, when seeking for the ring,
' How strange a wind is blowing on the door ! '

And said the old man, crouching to the fire :
' Draw close your chairs, for colder falls the night ;

Push fast the door, and pull the curtains to,
For it is dreary in the moon's pale light.'
And then his daughter's daughter with her hand
Passed over salt and clay to touch the ring,
Said low, 'The old need fire, but ah! the young
Have that within their heart to flame and sting.'

And then the spirit, moving from her place,
Touched there a shoulder, whispered in each ear,
Bent by the old man, nodding in his chair,
But no one heeded her, or seemed to hear.
Then crew the black cock, and so weeping sore
She went alone into the night again,
And said the greybeard, reaching for his glass,
'How sad a wind blows on the window-pane!'

And then from dreaming the long dreams of age
He woke, remembering, and let fall a tear:
'Alas! I have forgot—and have you gone?—
I set no chair to welcome you, my dear.'
And said the maidens, laughing in their play,
'How he goes groaning, wrinkled-faced and hoar,
He is so old, and angry with his age—
Hush! hear the banshee sobbing past the door.'

'I HAVE BEEN TO HY-BRASAIL' [1]

I HAVE been to Hy-Brasail,
And the Land of Youth have seen,
Much laughter have I heard there,
And birds amongst the green.

Many have I met there,
But no one ever old,
Yet I have left Hy-Brasail
Before my time was told.

Love have I known, too,
As I shall meet no more ;
Lost is the magic island,
And I cannot find the shore.

Since I have left Hy-Brasail,
Age has encompassed me,
She plucks me by the shoulder
And will not let me be.

[1] One of the Enchanted Isles, sometimes seen in the western
seas from the shores of Ireland.

Her face is grey and mournful,
Her hand is hard and cold,
Yet I have left Hy-Brasail
Before my time was told.

A CRY IN THE WORLD

KINE, kine in the meadows, why do you low so
  piteously?

High is the grass to your knees, and wet with the dew
  of the morn,

Sweet with the perfume of honey, and breath of the
  clover blossoms;

But the sad-eyed kine on the hillside see no joy in the
  day newborn.

'Man, man has bereft us and taken our young ones
  from us;

Thus we call in the eve, call through night to the
  break of day,

That they may hear and answer; so we find no
  peace in the meadows.

Our hearts are sad with hunger for the love man stole
  away.'

Bird, bird on the tree-top, my heart doth sigh for
  thy music;

In the glad air of morn and promise of summer,
  rejoice!

64

Thy head droops low on thy breast, half hid in thy
    ruffled feathers,
The grove is lone for thy singing, O bird of the
    silver voice !
' Man, man has bereft me, stolen my nestlings from me,
Wrecked the soft home we built 'mid the budding
    blossoms of spring.
My mate's brown wings grow red in vain beating the
    bars of her prison ;
With heart so full of longing and mourning, how can
    I sing ? '

Seal, in the cliff's shadow, why are thine eyes so
    mournful ?
Come from the gloom and the echo of the sea's sighs
    in the cave,
Sink down into deeper waters 'mid the hidden flowers
    of the ocean,
Or seek the splash and sparkle 'neath the snowy break
    of the wave.
' Man, man has bereft me, robbed me of those my
    loved ones ;
Alone, I find no gladness ; alone, where is joy for me
In the silvery flash of the fish or the wonderful
    gardens of coral ?
My eyes grow dim with watching the desolate waste
    of the sea ! '

E

Woman, king of the world is the babe you hush with
    sobbing,
King of all that is living in air or sea or on land,
Therefore, why do you kiss with lips that are dumb
    with sorrow?
Your tear-drops falling cold have chilled the little
    hand.
This is the soul's proud right, the earth given into his
    keeping;
And all that lives thereon must come to his feet a
    slave.
Mother, why do you flee with haggard eyes in the
    morning
To answer with white face hid in the grass of a
    baby's grave?

A FAIRY PRINCE

PRINCE CHARMING, when the wizard's wand
Had wrecked for aye my fairyland,
Had rased my castles to the earth,
And killed my child's heart with his mirth;
Then weeds grew rank where flowers had been,
And slow snakes flashed their length between.

Prince Charming, when the darkness came,
With many tears I called your name,
And 'Give me back my fairyland!'
You took me by the willing hand
Ere day had lit the dawn's pale flame;
You left me when the darkness came.

Prince Charming, spite of wizard's wand,
You said you'd find my fairyland.
I open eyes too sad for tears,
Nought but an open grave appears.

OUT WITH THE WORLD

I 'M out with all the world to-day,
So all the world to me is gray—
Ah me, the bonny world!
Glad birds are building in the tree,
For them I have no sympathy;
From out the grove a thrush pipes clear,
I have no wish his song to hear;
From tangled boughs that young buds share
With last year's leaves, a startled hare
A moment peeps and then away;
I have no laughter for his play,
For all the sunny sky is gray,
The weariest I am to-day
In all the weary world.
Perchance to-morrow's hidden store
May bring my heart's content once more.
The sweet young spring comes very fair
With summer's breath and golden air;

M

And I may think there cannot be
A maid so blest on land or sea.
I'm out, though, with the world to-day,
So all the world to me is gray—
Ah me, the bonny world!

THE LITTLE BROTHER

O BROTHER, brother, come down to the crags by the
      bay,
Come down to the caves where I play;
    For oh! I saw on the rocks, asleep,
    A fair mermaid, and the slow waves creep
To bear her away, away.

O brother, brother, come quick, till you laugh with
      me,
For no mermaid so fair is she,
    But the little lass that I saw last night
    (I hid in the shade, you stood in the light),
And she weeping so bitterly.

O brother, brother, I watched her through the day,
Saw her hair grow jewelled with spray;
    Once her cheek was brushed by a gull's wet wing,
    And a finch flew down on her hand to sing,
And was not afraid to stay.

O brother, brother, will she soon awakened be ?
I would that she laugh with me.
   She sleeps, and the world so full of sound—
   She's so deaf, like the dead that are under the
      ground,
That I laugh and laugh to see.

A WAYWARD ROSE

MISCHIEVOUS rose from the rose-tree swaying,
    Can I not bind thee nor hold thee?
    Can I not weave thee nor fold thee
In with thy sisters to staying?
Vain is my passion or praying,
Rose from the rose-tree swaying.

Wayward sweet rose from the rose-tree swinging,
    Can I not pass thee, forget thee?
    Can I not see to regret thee?
In—'mid thy kindred's close ringing,
Out—to my heart she comes winging,
Rose from the rose-tree swinging.

Cruel red rose from the rose-tree swaying,
    Ever to worship thee, throne thee,
    Never to lose thee nor own thee,
Thy beauty to keep me from straying,
Thy thorns for my passionate praying,
Rose from the rose-tree swaying.

MY ROSE

DROOP all the flowers in my garden,
  All their fair heads hang low,
For rose, their fairest companion
  Never again will they know.
Bring me no flowers for wearing,
  Take these strange buds away,
For I cannot now have the fairest :
  My rose that has died to-day.

What has blighted my blossom,
  Stricken it down with death,
Over the walls of my garden—
  What save the world's cold breath?
Then bring me no flowers for wearing,
  Take these strange buds away,
Since I cannot now have the sweetest :
  My rose that has died to-day.

IN WINTRY WEATHER

DEAR, in wintry weather,
How close we crept together!
The storms, with all their thunder,
Could not our fond hands sunder.
No sorrow followed after,
Cold words or scornful laughter.
How close we crept together,
Through all the wintry weather!

Dear, when each rose uncurled
To its sweet narrow world,
You went to cull their glory ;
You would not hear my story,
Too sweet the birds were singing,
Too fair the buds were swinging :
If I should come or go
You did not care to know.

When each sweet rose uncurled
To its unknown world,
How could you e'er remember
That in a bleak December,
Through all the bitter weather,
We crept so close together?

MONICA

PARDON give to Monica,
She is so very fair—
Though soft eyes give promises
Rosy lips forswear.
From the shy droop of her head
You a hope might take ;
In the hiding cheek, beware,
The dainty dimples wake.
Pardon give to Monica.

Pardon give to Monica,
The havoc of her eyes,
Yours they will not shun or seek,—
There the mischief lies.
If the flirting lashes thus
Make your day and night,
Would the loosing of your bonds
Give your heart respite ?
Pardon give to Monica.

Pardon give to Monica,
She is so very fair.
What those cruel lips may say,
Roguish eyes forswear.
What knight's heart amid ye all
Were not glad to break,
That the lips with pity droop,
While eyes their laughter take?
Pardon give to Monica.

A CARELESS HEART

The wind has blown my heart away
All on a summer holiday.
If you can find it, pray you tell,
For this is how the loss befell:

If you will now my tale believe,
I wore my heart upon my sleeve,
So came it that, alack the day!
The wind did blow my heart away.

THE FAIRIES

The fairies, the fairies, the mischief-loving fairies,
    Have stolen my loved one, my darling, and my dear ;
With charms and enchantments they lured and way-
        laid him,
    So my love cannot comfort and my presence can-
        not cheer.

The fairies, the fairies, I 'll love no more the fairies,
    I 'll never sweep the hearth for them nor care the
        fairy thorn ;
I 'll skim no more the yellow cream nor leave the
        perfumed honey,
    But I 'll drive the goats for pasture to their greenest
        rath each morn.

With Ave, and Ave, and many a Paternoster,
    Within their magic circle I 'll tell my beads for you ;
My prayers be sharp as arrows to pierce their soulless
        bosoms,
    Till they come with loud sorrow to tell me that they
        rue.

My darling, my darling, what glamour is upon you
  That you find for your gaze satisfaction and content
In the charms of that colleen, with her black, snaky
      ringlets,
  Her red lips contemptuous, and her gloomy brows
    so bent?

The fairies, the fairies, from her blue eyes were
      peeping;
  They blew her hair about you, so you were lost,
    my dear;
With their charms and enchantments they lured and
      waylaid you,
  So my love cannot comfort and my presence can-
    not cheer.

A ROSE WILL FADE

You were always a dreamer, Rose, red Rose,
    As you swung on your perfumed spray,
Swinging, and all the world was true,
Swaying, what did it trouble you?
    A rose will fade in a day.

Why did you smile to his face, red Rose,
    As he whistled across your way?
And all the world went mad for you,
All the world it knelt to woo.
    A rose will bloom in a day.

I gather your petals, Rose, red Rose,
    The petals he threw away.
And all the world derided you;
Ah! the world, how well it knew
    A rose will fade in a day!

LITTLE WHITE ROSE

LITTLE white rose that I loved, I loved,
    Roisin ban, Roisin ban !
Fair my bud as the morning's dawn.
I kissed my beautiful flower to bloom,
My heart grew glad for its rich perfume—
    Little white rose that I loved.

Little white rose that I loved grew red,
    Roisin ruad, Roisin ruad !
Passionate tears I wept for you.
Love is more sweet than the world's fame,—
I dream you back in my heart the same,
    Little white rose that I loved !

Little white rose that I loved grew black,
    Roisin dub, Roisin dub !
So I knew not the heart of you.
Lost in the world's alluring fire,
I cry in the night for my heart's desire,
    Little white rose that I loved !

INNOCENCE

White rose must die, all in the youth and beauty of the
    year,
Though nightingale should sing the whole night
    through,
Though summer breezes woo,
She will not hear.

Too delicate for the sun's kiss so hot and passionate,
Or for the rude caresses of the wind,
She drooped and pined—
They mourned too late.
Birds carol clear:
'Summer has come,' they say.
'O joy of living on a summer's day!'
White rose must die, all in the youth and beauty of the
    year.

SPRING SONG : TO IRELAND

WEEP no more, heart of my heart, no more !
    The night has passed and the dawn is here,
The cuckoo calls from the budding trees,
    And tells us that Spring is near.

Sorrow no more, beloved, no more !
    For see, sweet emblem of hope untold,
The tears that soft on the shamrocks fall
    There turn to blossoms of gold.

Winter has gone with his blighting breath,
    No more to chill thee with cold or fear,
The brook laughs loud in its liberty,
    Green buds on the hedge appear.

Weep no more, life of my heart, no more !
    The birds are carolling sweet and clear ;
The warmth of Summer is in the breeze,
    And the Spring—the Spring is here.

NEAR THE FORUM OF TRAJAN

In Rome, as I look from my lattice
    And lean to the night,
Where the living sleep, still as the dead are
    All in the sunlight.

The dead are awake 'mid our resting
    Beneath the pale moon.
I arise and will walk with their numbers,
    Dawn rises so soon.

I hear the bell voices together
    Crash into strange sound—
' I, Trajan, am cold '; I, Aurelius,
    Lie stiff in the ground.'

' Grey Cassius sleeps long, and grim Brutus,
    Proud Cæsar is dead ';
Thus the voices of time in their singing
    Roll over my head.

O spirits that throng me and whisper
    In desolate street,
O souls that so follow and mock me,
    You laugh and repeat :—

‘ Who is he who shouts into the silence
    More lone than us dead,
Who says he would walk with our numbers
    With echoing tread?

‘ Who would join in a world so immortal
    Yet touches no hand,
Why comes he, the child of the sunlight,
    To our haunted land?

‘ Would he know of our power and ambition,
    The worth of it all?
Let him seek the gold palace of Nero,
    And read on its wall.

‘ Let him look for our loves and desires
    In the palace of Kings,
Then bid him go hence with his living
    That tortures and stings.

‘ He is the ghost that would haunt us
    With dreams of past light ;
Drive him back to his kind in the sunshine,
    And leave us the night.’

AT POMPEII

At Pompeii I heard a woman laugh,
And turned to find the reason of her mirth,
Saw but the silent figure of a girl
That centuries had mummied into earth :

The running figure of a little maid
With face half-hidden in her shielding arm,
Silent, yet screaming, yea, in ev'ry limb,
The cruel torture of her dread alarm.

At Pompeii I heard a maiden shriek
All down the years from out the distant past ;
Blind in the awful darkness still she runs ;
Death in the mould of fear her form has cast.

A little maid once soft and sweet and white,
Full of the morning's hope, and love and joy,
That Nature, moving to the voice of Time,
Shook her dark wings to wither and destroy.

87

At Pompeii I saw a woman bend
Above this dead, pronounce an epitaph;
The mother of a child, it may have been.
Oh horrible! I heard a woman laugh.

Dora Sigerson

III

'THE ME WITHIN THEE BLIND!'

Then of the THEE IN ME *who works behind*
The Veil, I lifted up my hands to find
A lamp amid the Darkness, and I heard,
As from without—' THE ME WITHIN THEE BLIND!'
'Rubáiyát' of OMAR KHAYYÁM.
EDWARD FITZGERALD.

'THE ME WITHIN THEE BLIND!'

I

At the convent doors, full of alarm
She stood, like a young bird quitting its nest.
Her first flight flown right into my arm,
Her first tears wept upon my breast.
It was the young dove, wond'ring and afraid
To find the narrow circle of its home
Held not the forests in its ingle shade,
Held not the Heavens 'neath its simple dome.
Upon my heart she rested, finding so
A window to the world, and whisp'ring said,
'Your arms shall shield from evil winds that blow,
There from all sorrows I shall hide my head.
Your eyes my outlook to this wild'ring place
That I know nothing of, and you know all.'
So at my soul's dark windows pressed her face,
Saw there the world's first evil shadows fall.

She was not very learnèd, but all sweet,
All yielding, to a fault—exceeding kind.
A woman-child from dainty head to feet,
Too quick to act each impulse of her mind.
A lily grown within a holy place,
In air too pure the snowy bell uncurled
Ever the lashing winds of sin to face,
Or brave alone the knowledge of the world.
I set the blossom in the World's hot glare,
No walls to shelter it, no doors to keep
Its purity; I loved the crowd to stare,
Nor thought that time would change its snowy sleep.
A lamb it was, a little weakling one,
That I, the shepherd, took without its fold
And let—almost ere life was well begun—
The wolf get to, that tore it from my hold.

From out the walls that know not of men's love,
To meet her father's dying voice she flew,
Then turned to me—last friend the earth above—
She, loving little, thought she loved so true,
Wept long upon my breast, crept to my heart,
Became my wife, and lived in joy a while.
And then, as time went on, she drew apart,
I saw much tears and the less frequent smile,
The doubtful look the eyes had, bent on me,
As though some great illusion she had known.

And then, alas! I did not know nor see,
But now, too late, too plain the cause is shown.

Full of a quaint belief in God and man,
In prayers and miracles, and in all good,
The crystal fate of her pure teaching ran
Beneath my eyes, and was not understood.
I sullied the fair stream, for who was I
To meet a woman's eyes when up they steal
From gazing in the well where they descry
The dream reflection of a fair ideal?
A would-be cynic, and a man who had
No hope of Heaven, no belief in Hell,
To teach her of the world, its good and bad,
Why was it to his lot the teaching fell?
The little body, quickly satisfied,
Expressed no want I did not love to give—
I warmed it, clad it, fed it, yet denied
The larger soul within the right to live.
Her body would have loved me, been content
With my great worship, had her soul gone down
Beneath its living, but it fought and bent
The body to its will, till, with a frown
Of almost hate, she grew to see me come
To draw her to me in a fond embrace,
And kiss her lips, to all my kisses dumb.
And then I learned the anger of her face,

Spoke to her, questioned her, and got reply—
Not in these words, for she spake as a child,
Half full of anger, half inclined to cry,
Full of deep troubles, incoherent, wild.
But I have read their meaning to my heart,
Placed every thought, and speak them day by day,
Until I feel the sorrow and the smart
Will burn into my flesh when it is clay.

'I do not love you any more,' she said,
'Nor this great world.   Oh, I were better dead,
Or never born, for everything is wrong
I once thought good.   I am not brave nor strong
To understand and keep my weak soul white ;
It wanders from me to some dreadful night.
Before you took me, life was good and sweet,
Easy to understand and all complete ;
Within four walls we trod our daily way,
A holy life and love for each new day :
Sinless bright faces, purity and prayer,
A narrow life, yet oh, to me so fair !
But in your mighty world I do not know
Among its thousand ways the road to go ;
No great community doth wield the whole,
But many sects confront the seeking soul.
My wrong my neighbour's right, my joy his shame,
My tears his laughter, or my praise his blame.

Alas! if some sure haven I had found,
Or viewed the world from some near vantage-ground ;
But in your arms no shelter do I know
From all the blinding winds that round me blow.
Life was so fair to me, and death more sweet
With Heaven's joy, to make the crown complete.
But you, who had no God, have shut for me
The Heavens' gates, and bid me only see
A deaf, blind dome above me, and below
The wormy grave—I shudder as I go.

' Death was so sweet a dream, a meeting-place
Where we again should find each lost, dear face.
And all God's love, alas! for me no more,
But now the grave so dark I stand before.
Cold, black, and lonely my warm body's bed,
No prize for living—and for ever dead.
She too is gone, the Mary full of grace,
To me, a woman, took a mother's place,
Heard all the little griefs I dare not tell
To her dear Son.   To her a mother-maid
So comforting I went, all unafraid.

' Since God is lost, then all is lost indeed.
You did not know the comfort or the need
Of God for me, who am so frail and weak.
Blown by all winds, I know not where to seek.

Too busy with your books, you did not know
I stood beside you, and I suffered so,
For each vain question silenced with a kiss,
For each lost hope you did not pause to miss.
You did not hear my soul beside you cry,
' Look to me, friend ; your help, or else I die.'
Like some wayfarer on an Alpine height,
You with your glass would bring within your sight
And say, ' How soft he goes amidst the snow ! '
So smile upon him, for you could not know
That every mound a mountain was, and deep
Each velvet crevice—where the death-wolves creep
With purple jaws,—so that to fall or rest
Were but to die.   He struggles with despair,
While you beside your fire doth watch him there,
And say—' How soft he goes amidst the snow ! '
Wherein he battles, shrieking to the sky,
' O God, your pity, lest I faint and die ! '
I was a wife you had no time to woo,
I was a woman—and you never knew.
A child to you, because you could not hear
My woman's soul that called so loud and clear.
You thought that like a child I was afraid,
With all life's instinct, of the death you made
Me look to, and you kissed my tears away,
While I was weeping for the friends you say
I 'll see no more, and all the loss of those

Who never had been lost till you arose
To close God's gates and Heaven hide from me.
You gave me kisses, thinking I should be
As easy silenced as a child with sweets.
My soul will not be silent; it repeats
All the wise reasons that you bid me write
(I went with laughter, bidding you indite
For that great book of yours that went to prove
No Godhead bid the mighty world to move)
Against the probability of God.

' With your strong brain my weaker reason trod,
Until at last it followed step with you,
Beheld no God in all the starry blue.
And at my tears you smiled, and bid me go
Buy a new ring, a ribbon, or a bow.
I was too childish in my prayers, I see,
Now that all prayer has passed away from me.
Too much belief will make another go
Into too little, and 'twas even so
That I believed in God, and to my woe
Did not with reason temper my belief.
Your kindly humour, worse than biting scorn,
Smiled on my soul, till doubt at last was born
Better harsh words to drive my soul to bay
Continual laughter wore my faith away.

G

'When foolishly I first would make you come
Into the church, you knelt with heart all dumb.
You came to please me, weary of it all,
Until beside you I could hear the call
Your soul made at this mockery of prayer,
Till I too read your thoughts, and saw the glare
Of altar lights, as I had seen the flame
Of heathen worship.   And the priest who came
To serve his God, no longer seemed to me,
Being God's servant, more than man to be,
Saintlier, and purer, more than others are,
Who look on God's high altar from afar.
And reading thus your soul as you sat dumb,
I prayed again you would not seek to come.
And so you smiled, as though 'twas to your mind,
Saying belief sat well on womankind,
Fed their emotions, sentiments, and so
You loved a woman to a church to go,
But as I did not mind, you would remain
To write your book till I came home again.

'These were the little things doubt fattened on,
Until at last I found my faith had gone.
That day—I do remember all so well—
My baby died, I cried to God and fell
Down on my knees, and raised my eyes to you
For comfort from the horror that I knew.

I cried to God to let me meet again
My little one, where there was no more pain,
Only great love.   And ever by His feet
Each lost familiar face to see and greet.
And as I cried I turned and looked to you,
All dumbly praying you would say, "'Tis true,
That sweet old story.   There is no good-bye."
But your sad pitying eyes gave me the lie,
Saying he's dead, and there's no more than death.
I kissed the parted lips that had no breath,
So young to go into the dark alone,
Never to rise.   My heart seemed turned to stone,
And my soul dead.   Lest you should see my eyes
I looked through the dim window, and surprise
Dawned on me, for the world went by the same
As though behind our narrow wall the flame
Of life had not been quenched, and in its hair
The same sad wind of death blew even there,
Making the grey where once the gold had been,
Blew in its eyes, and all that they had seen
Was half forgotten.   Thus I stood and saw
The world go by, obeying some strange law
It knew not of, yet hurried to some goal
By this same death, that had us all in thrall.
And oh ! I seemed to see into each brain,
So busy with small thoughts, and all so vain,
Of petty fashions, plans for years to come—

Plans made for times when most their lips were
  dumb.
It seemed to me that death stood by my side
And smiled upon the crowd, well satisfied
To see them pass so gay, all fashion's slave.
And then I fell to thinking, even so
The world was ill and cruel, since my woe
Was all unwept for, that it drew not near
From out the sunshine once, to shed a tear,
But flitted by with laughter, and all gay,
Through the dim hours that tread their time away.
And so my heart cried to me : " Open wide
The doors of your sad house, and call inside
The passing crowd ; say, ' *Wherefore with such speed,*
Since here is what you haste to, death indeed ! ' "

' It was that night I dreamed the same sad dream,
That I upon a barren hill did seem
To watch the world go by in one great throng ;
As mountain winds will blow the leaves along,
By time's swift wind they ever hurried on ;
And as they passed their faces paled or shone
With fear or love of God.   And then I saw
That each poor, weary traveller did draw
A burden with him, and it seemed I knew
What was within the load that each one drew.
In one lay sorrow, in another pain,

In this stern duty done that bore no gain.
Here poverty was big, there bravely borne
Harsh words, then blows some weary back had torn.
So on, so on, but more with grief were bent
Than aught besides, tears did they bear content.
And when I closed my eyes a while to rest
From all these moving thousands, strangely blessed
With their sad loads, I looked again, and there
Beheld a figure, white, divinely fair,
Stretched on a cross, by hands that still were red
With dropping blood; and on the glorious head
A crown of thorns, while yet the eyes unclosed
Had not the glare of death's most chill repose,
But glowed yet with a love beyond man's power.

'And as I gazed, the people in the shower
Of His life's blood laid down their burdens there,
Departing whole, and with their faces fair,
"Through all the ages, living still," I cried,
"O Thou belovèd God!" And on the earth
I saw Faith move, and knew it had its birth
As soon as Time, and all beneath the sun
Drew comfort from their Gods—that were but One,
The only God, though served in many ways.
And as I prayed, I heard to my amaze
Long laughter, hard and loud, that shook and spread
Around, above us, over every head

In that vast crowd, that shuddered, fell apart
Before the mockery, and in my heart
Cold horror grew.   I turned to seek the cause
Of that strange humour—coming without pause,
And there, upon a little hill, beheld
A man, face hid in hands, whose laughter swelled
Above all cries.   "Wherefore," I said, "you dare
Disturb the people, busy with their prayer?
What do you see to move your laughter so?"
"I see," he said, "a multitude, that go
All full of prayer, yet laden down with grief,
With pain and tears, yet, such is their belief,
The load is light."   And so he laughed again.
"And is your mirth," I said, "at joy or pain?"
"I laugh to see them come and pray," he said,
"To pray, and pray, and pray, when God is dead."
And as he spoke, the people, parting, fell
Into confusion, underneath the spell
Of his loud laughter, and beneath the Cross
Came sounds of strife; he laughed, "Behold the loss
Of Him who never was."   I looked, and there,
Still nailed, a wooden God the tree did bear.
And then the crowd slow-drifting crept away,
All deeply laden; I alone did stay,
Hearing their parting cries, as on and on
Into the dust that hid them they were gone.
And then he spoke, when all had passed us by,

"They are but as the leaves that fall and fly;
Blown by the winds of time, they on are borne
To separate, and from each other torn
To fade apart, to wither there and die."
And as he laughed, I gave a bitter cry
And sprang to stop him; raising up a stone
To slay him with, I vowed he should atone
For this black horror, in a holy place.
He raised his head—O God, he had your face!'

And here she ended all the bitter tale,
And I, poor fool, no word could find to speak,
But let her go, with little face all pale,
And heavy sobbing like her heart would break.
I was so angry, finding all my care
And all my love as nothing in her sight,
I had forgotten that the larger share
Was in my heart, and never saw the light.
I was too old to act a lad's gay part,
To hang upon her words, be by her side
All the long day, yet oh! within my heart
She had no rival since she was my bride,
Save those same books, that did divorce indeed
Her love for me.   Ah, would that I had torn
Them leaf from leaf, and so destroyed my creed,
Before they caused that gentle heart to mourn!
Would I had thrown myself down at her feet,

And learnèd there the simple faith she knew,
Not by a sneer the every sign to meet,
And pierce the gentle soul thus through and through!
Would I had caught her as she passed me then,
All full of tears, and flung my book away,
And vowed no more to wound her with my pen—
What grief was brought me for that brief delay!
Oh, what was fame, that I should sacrifice
My love's sweet soul to catch the world's vain ear—
More joy, indeed, to keep the heart I prize
Above all fame, beside me ever dear.
But I with sullen look let her pass by,
And did not speak when last she turned her head,
Nor when beside the door I heard a sigh
Breathing farewell, although my own heart bled.
'Good-bye,' 'Good-bye,' I hear it night and day,
Always with tears, and then the whisper low,
'I do not care now what I do or say,
There is no right, and I am glad to go.'
She glad to go!—I did not heed her speech
Until, all tired of anger, I had gone
Into her room, a pardon to beseech,
And found the bed had not been pressed upon,
And it so late.   All through the empty room
And through the house I searched for her in vain,
And staggered, like a man to meet his doom,
Out in the darkness to the storm and rain,

And there I ran and called to her till dawn.
Like some mad thing, I hunted through the night,
Until the glowing stars that on me shone
Withdrew in pity, giving me the light.
Sane with the morning, home I sought once more,
My home to me now ever desolate;
But day, alas! did not my peace restore,
And bring her back in love, who left in hate.

'Good-bye,' 'Good-bye,' 'and I am glad to go,'
O God! those words that echo down the years,
To drop upon my heart in endless woe,
With all the bitter hopelessness of tears.
Gone, gone!—how did they ever pass,
The lone, long months, the endless weeks and days,
The wingèd hopes that flew from me, alas,
And left me helpless in a stunned amaze!
Gone, gone, for ever gone!—a ghost stole by
Within my house to dwell, and met me there,
Behind each open door to peep and fly,
And look upon me from her empty chair;
Sweet ghost it was, that had no face but hers.
One time I thought her fingers brushed my cheek,
Thinking she had returned all unawares,
Reached up to hold her, half afraid to speak—
Reached up, and found within my eager hand
A withered leaf blown through the open door;

And then again I seemed to see her stand,
And hear the sobbing of her voice once more.
'We are but as the leaves that fall and fly,
Blown by the wind of time they on are borne,
To fade apart, to wither there and die,
To separate, each from the other torn.'
Oh, the long days!—I could not stay nor go
By my lone house, but like a maddened thing
Would dream some time she, wounded, home might
    stray
Like some lost dove upon a broken wing.
Like some poor bird robbed of its nestling, I
Would hasten home to find it cold and drear,
Again fly forth, because some hidden cry
Would seem her voice that called in trouble near.
Oh, the long hours of sorrow and of gloom
'Neath the snow-lifting curtain of the night,
When each black hour might be her stroke of doom.
And every second make her deadly plight!

Did I then ever sleep, or was my dream
So like to waking that there seemed to be
No slaking of my anguish! In the stream
Of drowning thoughts there was no hope for me.
'I do not care now what I do,' she said.
O God! I trembled, seeking in the night,
Did she guess at her dangers, so untried,

What did she dream of in her desperate flight?
I do believe in hell, I do believe
In all its tortures.   I have known great grief
As few men know it, nor did I receive
Or for a moment gain a prayer's relief.
But through the night I wander, damned, alone,
With Hell's despair high flaming in my breast,
My every hope long turned into a stone ;
And yet I go, still seeking without rest.

Once, crouching in the shadow of my hall
I saw a woman raise her hand to ring.
Eager with hope I hurried—heard her fall
To drunken weeping, then begin to sing.
Cold with this horror, out into the night
I ran and wandered through the streets till morn ;
And once again between me and the light
I saw one pass—and hope again was born.
Slow did I follow, till my foolish heart
Leaped up and claimed her, so I took her hand,
To meet a stranger's eyes, and feel her start,
Surprised at grief she could not understand.
For one brief moment did the womanhood,
Half quenched in her, look forth with pity sweet,
As though a sorrow once she understood—
Then mocking laughter echoed through the street
And left me broken, adding to my hell

Another torture.   Could I live and know
My child was out amongst these fiends to dwell,
Her small, lost feet went straying to and fro?

All the cold river did I walk beside,
Thinking her face would some time meet my eyes
White on some dark wave pillow, but the tide
Lay dull and silent till the grey sunrise.
Once did I see a little form all bent
Go by the water, creeping in the shade,
As though the last small grain of hope were spent,
And all were lost, the debtor still unpaid.
She flung herself upon a bench at last,
Her thin face hidden in a shaking hand;
My soul cried to her when I would have passed,
I knelt beside her, by my grief unmanned.
I called one name, I raised her drooping head,
My hands, wet with her tears, lay on her cheek.
'Beloved!' I cried, she thrust me off and fled
Before the words my heart had made me speak,
But not before her face I saw, and knew
She was not my lost love, but one so sad,
So lost to hope, that I should track her too,
Or solitude and grief would make her mad.
But when I tried to seek her, she had passed
Into the whirling world, to tread alone
Life's bitter fruit, and drain the wine at last

Whose every drop will burn her heart to stone.
O women, women, in these awful nights
I learned the cruel burden which is yours!
Thrust from the giddy world of dear delights
Into the dark, she suffers and endures.
Tender, you are not fit for such a fight
Or such a foe as man can be to you.
God pity those who wander in the night,
And have no star of love to guide them through!

And oh! God pity me who may not know
Where go her straying feet by night or day,
When each long mile I eagerly do go
May bear me from her yet more far away!
God pity me, who in the night awake
Do fear the cruel laughter of the town
And women's cries,—the echoing feet, who make
Life's bitter struggle ere they sink, go down.

II

To-night I found her; fate was kind to me;
For one brief hour I had her once again,
And her dear face once more was blessed to see,
Although my voice did call to her in vain.
Back to her convent home she had returned,

Walked many miles, and fell before the door,
All weary save the brain that throbbed and burned,
And restless fever through her pulses tore.
There was she found, and borne into the home
She left all full of eager hopes, and gay
With life's young innocence that loved to roam,
And fell by thieves upon the world's highway.
Robbed of all joys, and whipped by time and care,
This poor wayfarer had once more gone back
To that lost home she once remembered fair,
To seek her jewels on the homeward track.
And so I found her.   Sitting by her bed,
I marvelled greatly how she ever came
So many miles, for yet her soft feet bled,
And bitter hardship marred her tender frame.
I may not ever know what she has borne
Through these long days when she was lost to me,
But oh! the bitterest grief I have to mourn
Are those most cruel trials I did not see—
Are those sad, unseen tears, whose track remained
In her sad eyes that did not rest in sleep,
Are those unknown afflictions, marked and stained
On the small hands she did not let me keep.
I heard her fevered lips call on the dead
In loving cries that through her bosom tore,
And then, repeating all the words I said
Of resurrection, fall to weeping sore.

And then she sobbed : 'Death stands here by my side,
And my sad soul is all afraid to go,
Because the hope of Heaven is still denied.
What bears the darkness yet I cannot know ;
I would be brave if I could overcome
The evil thoughts that follow me and cry,
All in my ears, that Heaven itself is dumb,
And death be mine for ever when I die.'

And so, to soothe her, spoke my tortured voice,
Breathing a poem that once she loved and knew,
How in death's anguish shall the soul rejoice,
And joy be hers when last she struggles through.
And ' Oh,' I said, ' some time I too shall see
" *Peace out of pain*," " *a light*," and "*then thy breast*."
Safe in my arms, belovèd, you shall be
In long embrace, "*and with God be the rest*." '
And hearing me with her bewildered brain,
She caught the verses with a sudden smile,
And ' *One fight more*,' she quotes the verse again,
' *The last and best*,' she quiet lay a while,
And then she spoke more calmly than before:
' I was a dreamer, and I 'll dream again,
One dream, the last and best, the first and last.
Death blesses me the dream I can retain,
My first sweet dream, the evil time is past.
The dream that made the world a joyful place,

Worth being born for, strong one's load to bear,
Easy to live, easy to fight and face,
To suffer all its tortures and its care.
Death shall not conquer me. I will not die
In his cold land, but fly to some embrace
In that belovèd sphere, where my one cry
Can summon to my aid an angel's face.
I will not die.'   And then she turned to me,
And peace and sanity shone in her eyes,
As though at last my face she chanced to see.
I hid it from her, seeking a disguise,
For fear she still did hate me, but she said,
As though the first days were, 'And have you
    come?
You were so long!' then heavy leaned her head
Upon my shoulder, and her lips were dumb.

Thus did I lose her for a second time,
Now without hope of meeting.   In my grief
I go from church to church, from clime to clime,
A lone man, damnèd by his unbelief.

IV

THE WOMAN WHO WENT TO HELL

(AN IRISH LEGEND)

A prose version of this ballad, to
which the author is indebted, will
be found in Mr. William Larminie's
West Irish Folk-Tales and Romances.

THE WOMAN WHO WENT TO HELL

AN IRISH LEGEND

Young Dermod stood by his mother's side,
And he spake right stern and cold:
' Now, why do you weep and wail,' he said,
' And joy from my love withhold?

' And why do you keen and cry,' said he,
' So loud on my marriage-day?
The wedding-guests, they all eager wait
Still clad in their rich array.

' The priest is ready with book and stole,
And you do this grievous thing:
You keep me back from the altar rail—
My bride from her wedding-ring.'

His mother, she rose, and she dried her tears,
She took him by his right hand—
' The cause,' she said, ' of my grief and pain,
Too soon must you understand.

115

'Oh, one-and-twenty long years ago
I walked in your father's farm,
I broke a bough from a ripe peach-tree,
And carried it on my arm.

'My heart was light as a thistle-seed—
—I had but been wed a year—
I dreamt of a joy that would soon be mine—
A babe in my arms so dear.

'There came to me there a stranger man,
And these are the words he spake :
"Now, all you carry I fain would buy,
I pray you my gold to take."

'And all I carried he then did buy—
You lying beneath my heart—
I tended to him the ripe fruit bough,
He tore the bright branch apart.

'He whispered then in my frightened ear
The name of the Evil One.
"And this have I bought to-day," he said—
"The soul of your unborn son.

'"The fruit you carry, which I did buy,
Will ripen before I claim ;

And when the bells of his wedding ring,
Again shall you hear my name."'

Now Dermod rose from his mother's side,
And all loud and long laughed he ;
He bore her down to the wedding-guests,
All sorrowful still was she.

'Now cry no more, sweet mother,' he said,
'For you are a doleful sight.
Now who is here in the banquet-hall
Can claim my soul to-night?'

Then one rose up from the wedding throng,
But his face no man could see,
And he said : 'Now bid your dear farewell,
For your soul belongs to me.'

Young Dermod stood like a stricken man,
His mother she swooned away ;
But his love ran quick to the stranger's side,
And to him she this did say :—

'If you will let his young soul go free,
I will serve you true and well,
For seven long years to be your slave
In the bitterest place of hell.'

'Seven long years if you be my slave
I will let his soul go free.'
The stranger drew her then by the hand
And into the night went he.

Seven long years did she serve him true
By the blazing gates of hell,
And on every soul that entered in
The tears of her sorrow fell.

Seven long years did she keep the place,
To open the doors accurst;
And every soul that her tear-drops knew—
It would neither burn nor thirst.

And once she let in her father dear,
And once her brother through;
Once came a friend she had loved full well,
Oh, bitter it was to do!

On the last day of the seven long years
She stood by her master's knee—
'A boon, a boon for the work well done,
I pray that you grant to me;

'A boon, a boon that I carry forth,
What treasure my strength can bring.'

' *That* you may do,' said the Evil One,
' And all for a little thing.'

' All you can carry you may take forth
By serving me seven years more.'
Bitter she wept for the world and love,
But took her sad place by the door.

Seven long years did she serve him well,
Until the last day was done ;
And all the souls that she had let in,
They clung to her one by one.

And all the souls that she had let through
They clung to her dress and hair,
Until the burden that she brought forth
Was heavy as she could bear.

The first who stopped her upon her way
Was a maiden all fair to see,
And, ' Sister, your load is great,' she said,
' So give it, I pray, to me.'

' Mary I am ; God sent me forth
That you to your love might go.'
The woman she drew the maid's robe aside
And a cloven hoof did show.

'And I will not give it to you,' she said,
Quick clasping her burden tight ;
And all the souls that surrounded her
Clung closer in dire affright.

The next who stopped her upon her way
Was an angel with sword aflame :
'The Lord has sent for your load,' he said.
'Saint Michael it is my name.'

The woman drew back his gown of white,
And the cloven hoof did see :
'Oh ! God be with me to-night,' she said,
'For bitter my sorrows be.

'And I will not give it to you,' said she,
And wept full many a tear ;
And all the souls that her burden made
Cried out in desperate fear.

The third who met her upon her way
Was a man with face so fair,
She knelt her down at His wounded feet,
And she laid her burden there.

'Oh, I will give it to you,' she said,
And fell in a swoon so deep,

The flying souls and their cries of joy
Did not waken her from her sleep.

Seven long days did her slumber last,
And oh but her dream was sweet!
She thought she wandered in God's far land,
The bliss of her hopes complete.

And when she woke on the seventh day,
To her love's home did she go,
And there she met neither man nor maid
Who ever her face did know.

And lo! she saw set a wedding-feast,
And tall by her own love's side
There leaned a maiden all young and fair
Who never should be his bride.

'A drink, a drink, my little page-boy,
A drink I do pray you bring';
She took the goblet up in her hand
And dropped in her golden ring.

'He who would marry, my little page,
I pray that he drink with me
To the old true love that he has forgot,
And this must his toasting be.'

When her false lover had got the cup,
He drained it both deep and dry:
'To my dead love that I mourned so long,
And I would that she now were nigh!'

He took from the cup the golden ring,
And he turned it in his hand ;
He said, ' Whoever has sent this charm,
I cannot her power withstand.'

'Oh, she is weary, and sad, and old,'
The little page-boy replied ;
But Dermod strode through the startled guests,
And stood by his own love's side.

He took her up in his two strong arms,
And, ' Have you come home ? ' he said ;
' Twice seven long years I mourned you well
As silent among the dead.'

He kissed her twice on her faded cheek
And thrice on her snow-white hair,
' And this is my own true wife,' he said,
To the guests who gathered there.

' Oh, she is withered and old,' they cried,
' And her hair is pale as snow ;

'Twere better you take the fair young girl,
And let the sad old love go.'

'I will not marry the fair young girl,
No woman I wed but this ;
The sweet white rose of her cheek,' said he,
'Shall redden beneath my kiss.

'There is no beauty in all the land
Who can with her face compare.'
He led her up to the table-head
And set her beside him there.

c 1

Printed by T. and A. Constable, Printers to Her Majesty
at the Edinburgh University Press